هَلولای دریا !

Sea Monster

Sedigheh Javidi

AuthorHouse™ UK
1663 Liberty Drive
Bloomington, IN 47403 USA
www.authorhouse.co.uk
Phone: 0800.197.4150

Published by AuthorHouse 10/09/2018

ISBN: 978-1-5462-9928-8 (sc)
ISBN: 978-1-5462-9927-1 (e)

Print information available on the last page.

authorHOUSE®

Sea Monster

The fishes were partying. It was the fourteenth day of the month. The moon was shining like a silver pond in the sky. Her beautiful rays were spreading out on the heart of the sea. It was springtime. The gentle breeze was sparking small waves in the water. The waves were crawling on each other and were moving forward. Little fishes were playing hide and seek between waves.

Tiny fish was hiding. His friends were looking for him. Tiny fish jumped and hit his fins to the water and flew like a baby sparrow in the air. Water fell on his shining scales and the moonlight shone his body like a shining star.

When he was flying joyfully in the air he suddenly saw the bottom of the sea. He got surprised he has never seen it. Lots of beautiful colors were sprayed on water. Its beauty spelled him. So fascinated he was that he forgot he was playing hide and seek.

He couldn't breathe so he jumped back to water. Little fishes gathered around him and rejoice. It was first time they were the winners.

The sky was filled with stars and jellyfishes lanterns became bright. Tiny fish mom putted him to sleep in his shelly cradle. Mommy fish knew lots of beautiful stories that she learned from her mother. The mermaid story, white whale's story, coral spell's story and even story of sea monster .That night Mommy fish told lots of stories but tiny fish couldn't sleep. He was still dreaming about the colors in water that he didn't know where they coming from.

Tiny fish: If I dive in those colors and jump in the sky .... How beautiful I would be

Mommy fish slept. The bubbles coming out of her month were getting smaller. Tiny fish looked at his mother. He slowly got out of his cradle and reached to water surface. Water was warm and clear and it smelled good .tiny fish looked around him. He had to go.

He went and went until he reached a cliff where a strange thing was sitting on it.

Tiny fish thought it's the sea monster.

Tiny fish: Hello! Are you the sea monster?

The old turtle opened the corner of his eyes.

Tiny fish: You will eat me?

The turtle laughed.

Tiny fish: there are lots of beautiful colors on the water, have you see them?

Turtle: They are not colors kid. They are lights.

Tiny fish got surprised and said: "but there are not white …. If I go there my scales will be colorful. It's so cool isn't it?"

The turtle sadly said: "No."

Tiny fish was so excited that he didn't hear the turtle answer and dived under water.

The turtle panicky screamed: "Don't go, sea monster is there."

The turtle sighed and watched the tiny fish moving away. He remembered the old days. If he had listened to his mother and did not go to the colorful lights, this ring would not get stuck around his waist and it won't hurt this much.

Turtle: god save you little fish.

It was near dawn. Stars were getting lost. A straight line was drawn on the water. Tiny fish rushed and dived under water. His fins were moving fast and pushing him forward. Water was getting colder and tasted bad. Tiny fish pulled his head out of water. He was terrified. The colors on water were no more. He couldn't see well, it was as if there was dust in front of his eyes, smell of water was making it hard for him to breath.

A voice: tiny fish ...... tiny fish .....

The voice was coming from a bottle; a silver sardine was stuck in the bottle.

Sardine: Can you help me out?

Tiny fish wondered and asked: "What are you doing in there?"
Then he took the sardine's fins and pulled her out.
Tiny fish: I'm looking for colors on the water. Did you see them?

Sardine laughed and said: "They are lights. In the morning, the beach lights are off, and you can't find them anymore. It's very dangerous there. You have to go back."

Tiny fish: Why?
Sardine said: "Cause sea monster is there. Also it's full of trash and no fish can breathe there and there is no food. Look, the color of water is changed. Humans pour their dirty waters in the sea."
Tiny fish angrily said: "How rude!"

Sardine: Do you see that black smoke there? It's a factory. Water in there is so hot that it can boil you.

Tiny fish fearfully said: "Oh no!"

Sardine: I was getting out of here but I got stuck in this bottle.

Tiny fish anxiously asked: "What should we do now?"

Sardine said: "we should wait until night so we can find our way back home"

The news of loss of tiny fish soon arrived to emperor of sea and dolphin. The Emperor of the Sea was a swordfish who knew all the sea routes and was so powerful that he could easily break the fisherman's fishing nets.

The kind dolphin was also the smartest marine creature in sea and was always ready to help others.

The jellyfish said: "I will also come. I can light your way in deep waters darkness."

The Seahorse said: "I will also come. I can walk on water and look for tiny fish."

The flounder said: "I should come too. I can paralyze our enemies and also I can fly and look for tiny fish."

Mommy fish was very worried. She guessed that he had gone to the colored lights. She knew that they should find him before it's too late. The old turtle saw the fishes that are looking for tiny fish and apprehensively said: "He went that way .... Hurry..."

The fishes rushed to the beach. The sun had reached the middle of the sky. Tiny fish had his head out of water and he was waiting. Suddenly the flounder saw him.

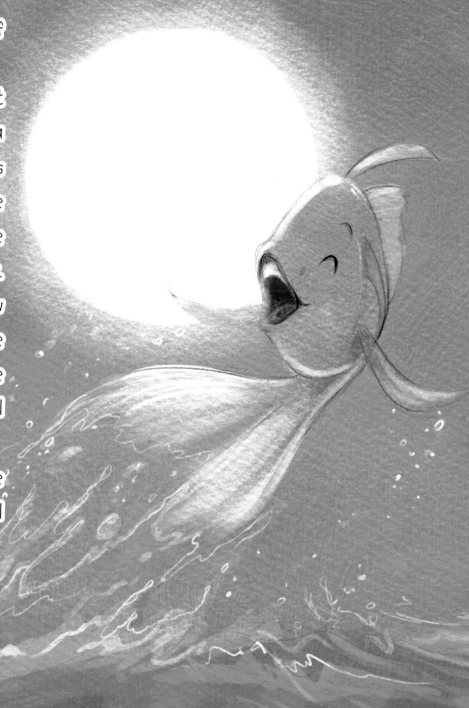

It was the fifteenth night of the month.

The moon was thinner but it was still shining like a silver pond in the sky. It was springtime. Tiny fish, sardine and other little fishes were playing under moonlight. Tiny fish jumped and flew like a baby sparrow in the air. On the other side of the sea there were beautiful lights spreading on sea.

Tiny fish now knows: "Some things are only beautiful from distance."

Printed in the United States
By Bookmasters